GUARDIANS OF THE GALAXY

ROCKET RACCOON™ #3

A CHASING TALE PART THREE

MARVEL
marvelkids.com
© MARVEL

ABDO
Spotlight

ABDOPUBLISHING.COM

Reinforced library bound edition published in 2018 by Spotlight,
a division of ABDO, PO Box 398166, Minneapolis, Minnesota 55439.
Spotlight produces high-quality reinforced library bound editions for
schools and libraries. Published by agreement with Marvel Characters, Inc.

Printed in the United States of America, North Mankato, Minnesota.
042017
092017

THIS BOOK CONTAINS
RECYCLED MATERIALS

marvelkids.com
© 2017 MARVEL

PUBLISHER'S CATALOGING IN PUBLICATION DATA

Names: Young, Skottie, author. | Young, Skottie ; Beaulieu, Jean-Francois ; Parker,
    Jake, illustrators.
Title: Rocket Raccoon / writer: Skottie Young ; art: Skottie Young ; Jean-Francois
    Beaulieu ; Jake Parker.
Description: Reinforced library bound edition. | Minneapolis, Minnesota : Spotlight,
    2018. | Series: Guardians of the galaxy : Rocket Raccoon | Volumes 1, 2, 3, and
    4 written by Skottie Young ; illustrated by Skottie Young & Jean-Francois
    Beaulieu. | Volumes 5 and 6 written by Skottie Young ; illustrated by Skottie
    Young , Jake Parker & Jean-Francois Beaulieu.
Summary: Rocket's high-flying life of adventure is at stake when he's framed for
    murder, and with an imposter one step ahead of him, and various terminators
    tracking him, can Rocket make it out alive and clear his name?
Identifiers: LCCN 2017931597 | ISBN 9781532140846 (#1: A Chasing Tale Part
    One) | ISBN 9781532140853 (#2: A Chasing Tale Part Two) | ISBN
    9781532140860 (#3: A Chasing Tale Part Three) | ISBN 9781532140877 (#4: A
    Chasing Tale Part Four) | ISBN 9781532140884 (#5: Storytailer) | ISBN
    9781532140891 (#6: Misfit Mechs)
Subjects: LCSH: Superheroes--Juvenile fiction. | Adventure and adventurers--
    Juvenile fiction. | Comic books, strips, etc.--Juvenile fiction. | Graphic novels--
    Juvenile fiction.
Classification: DDC 741.5--dc23
LC record available at https://lccn.loc.gov/2017931597

Spotlight

A Division of ABDO
abdopublishing.com

MARVEL ENTERTAINMENT PROUDLY PRESENTS

ROCKET

GUARDIAN OF THE GALAXY, TERRIBLE BOYFRIEND, INTERGALACTIC FUGITIVE?!

ROCKET HAS ALWAYS THOUGHT HE WAS THE LAST OF HIS KIND, BUT IT LOOKS LIKE ANOTHER RACCOON IS OUT THERE KILLING PEOPLE AND ROCKET JUST WON'T STAND FOR IT.

IN ORDER TO PROVE HIS INNOCENCE, ROCKET TURNED HIMSELF IN AND DEMANDED TO BE SENT TO THE MOST DANGEROUS PRISON PLANET IN THE GALAXY: DEVIN-9!

TURNS OUT ONE OF THE PRISONERS THERE, AN OLD PAL OF ROCKET AND GROOT'S NAMED MACHO GOMEZ, COULD GET THEM IN TOUCH WITH FUNTZEL, AN INTERGALACTIC KINGPIN, WHO'LL KNOW WHAT THE HECK IS GOIN' ON.

EN ROUTE TO FUNTZEL, THOUGH, THE TRIO ENCOUNTERED THE EX-TERMINATORS, A MYSTERIOUS GROUP THAT WANTS ROCKET DEAD.

GET IN LINE, LADIES!

RACCOON
A CHASING TALE PART THREE

skottie young
words and art

jean-françois beaulieu
color art

jeff eckleberry
lettering

skottie young
cover art

pascal campion
variant cover

irene y. lee
production

devin lewis
assistant editor

sana amanat
editor

nick lowe
senior editor

axel alonso
editor in chief

joe quesada
chief creative officer

dan buckley
publisher

alan fine
executive producer

MARVEL
marvelkids.com
© MARVEL

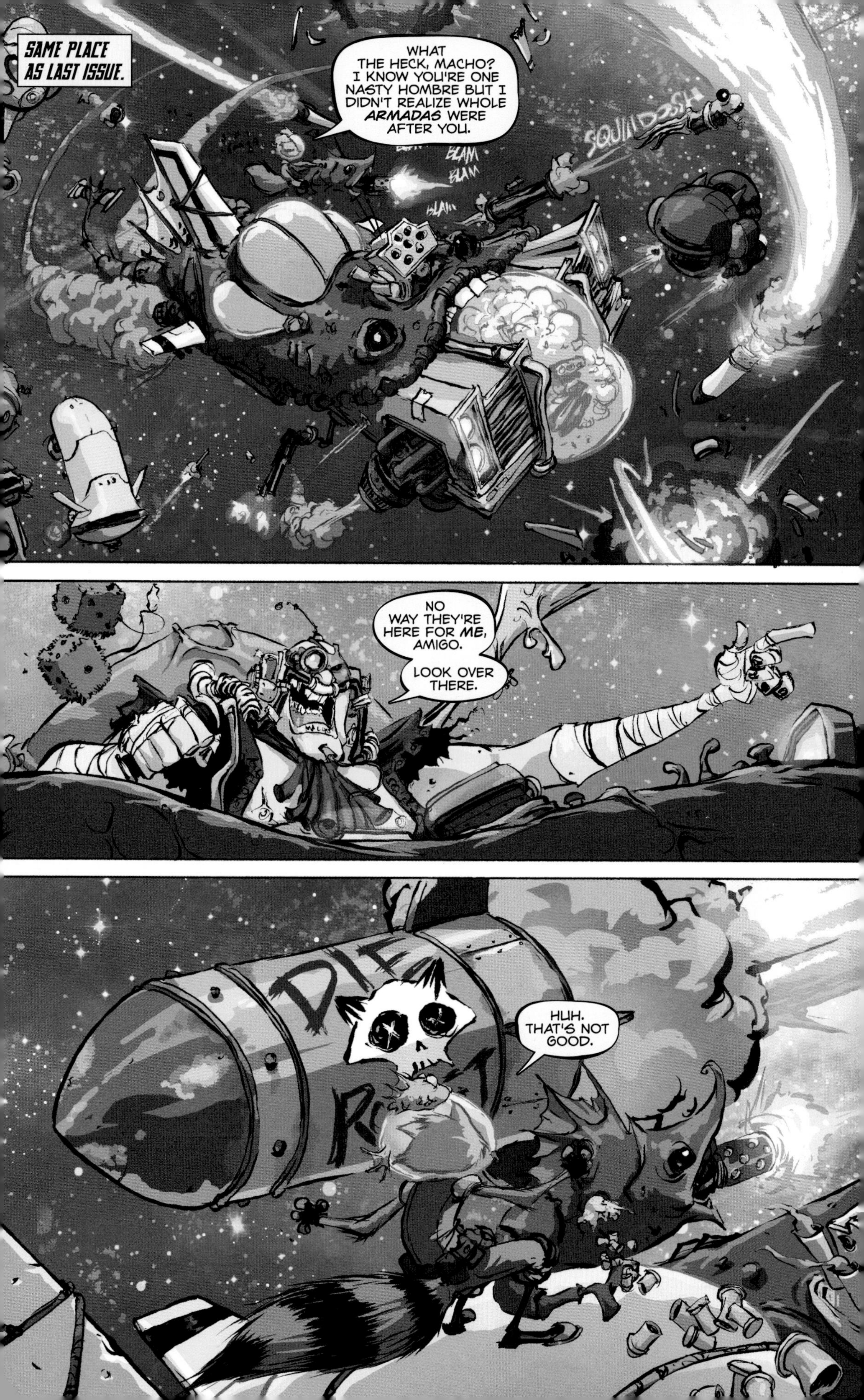
SAME PLACE AS LAST ISSUE.
WHAT THE HECK, MACHO? I KNOW YOU'RE ONE NASTY HOMBRE BUT I DIDN'T REALIZE WHOLE ARMADAS WERE AFTER YOU.
SQUIIDOOSH
BLAM
BLAM
NO WAY THEY'RE HERE FOR ME, AMIGO.
LOOK OVER THERE.
DIE
HUH. THAT'S NOT GOOD.

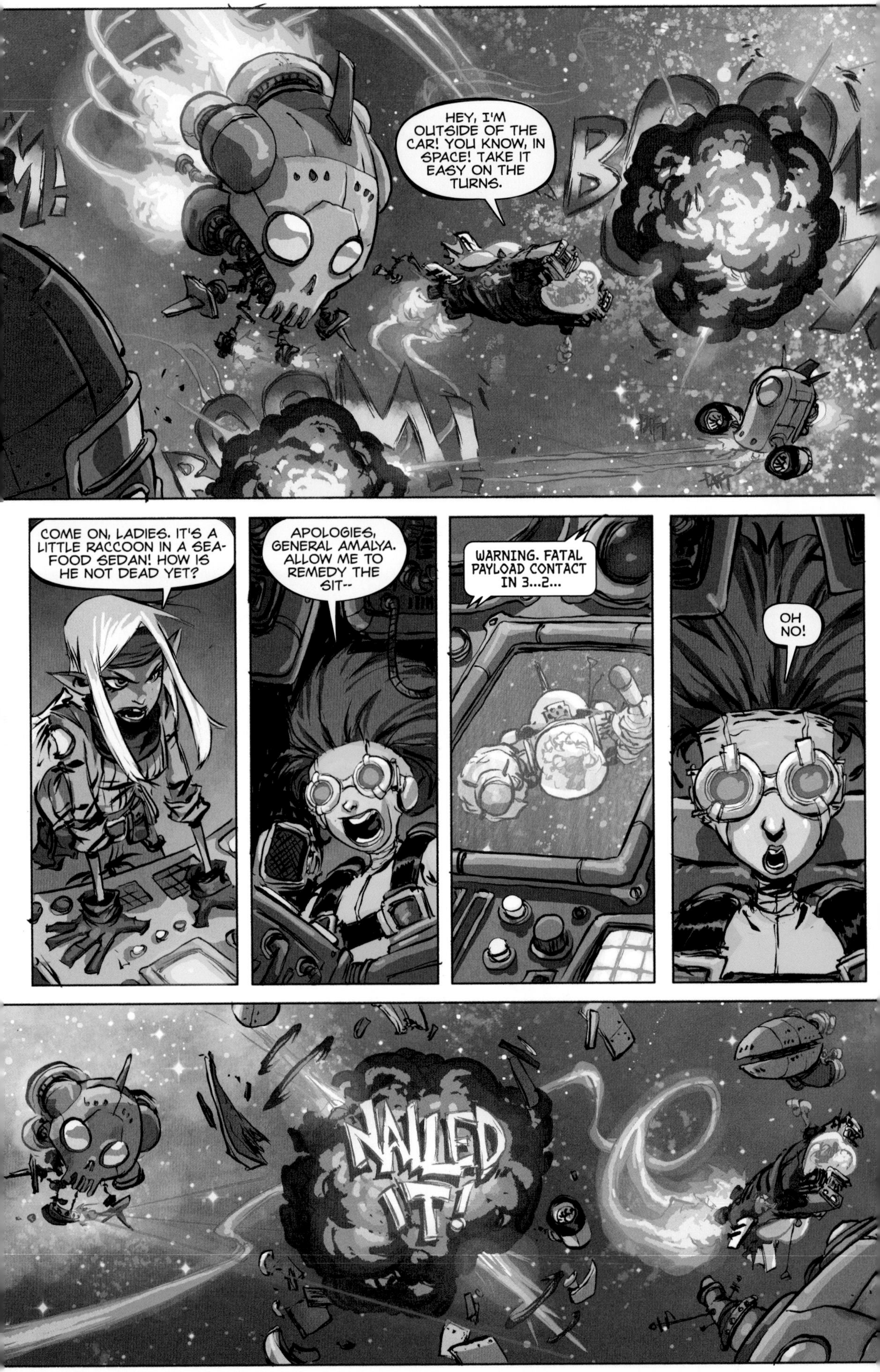
HEY, I'M OUTSIDE OF THE CAR! YOU KNOW, IN SPACE! TAKE IT EASY ON THE TURNS.
COME ON, LADIES. IT'S A LITTLE RACCOON IN A SEA-FOOD SEDAN! HOW IS HE NOT DEAD YET?
APOLOGIES, GENERAL AMALYA. ALLOW ME TO REMEDY THE SIT--
WARNING. FATAL PAYLOAD CONTACT IN 3...2...
OH NO!
NAILED IT!

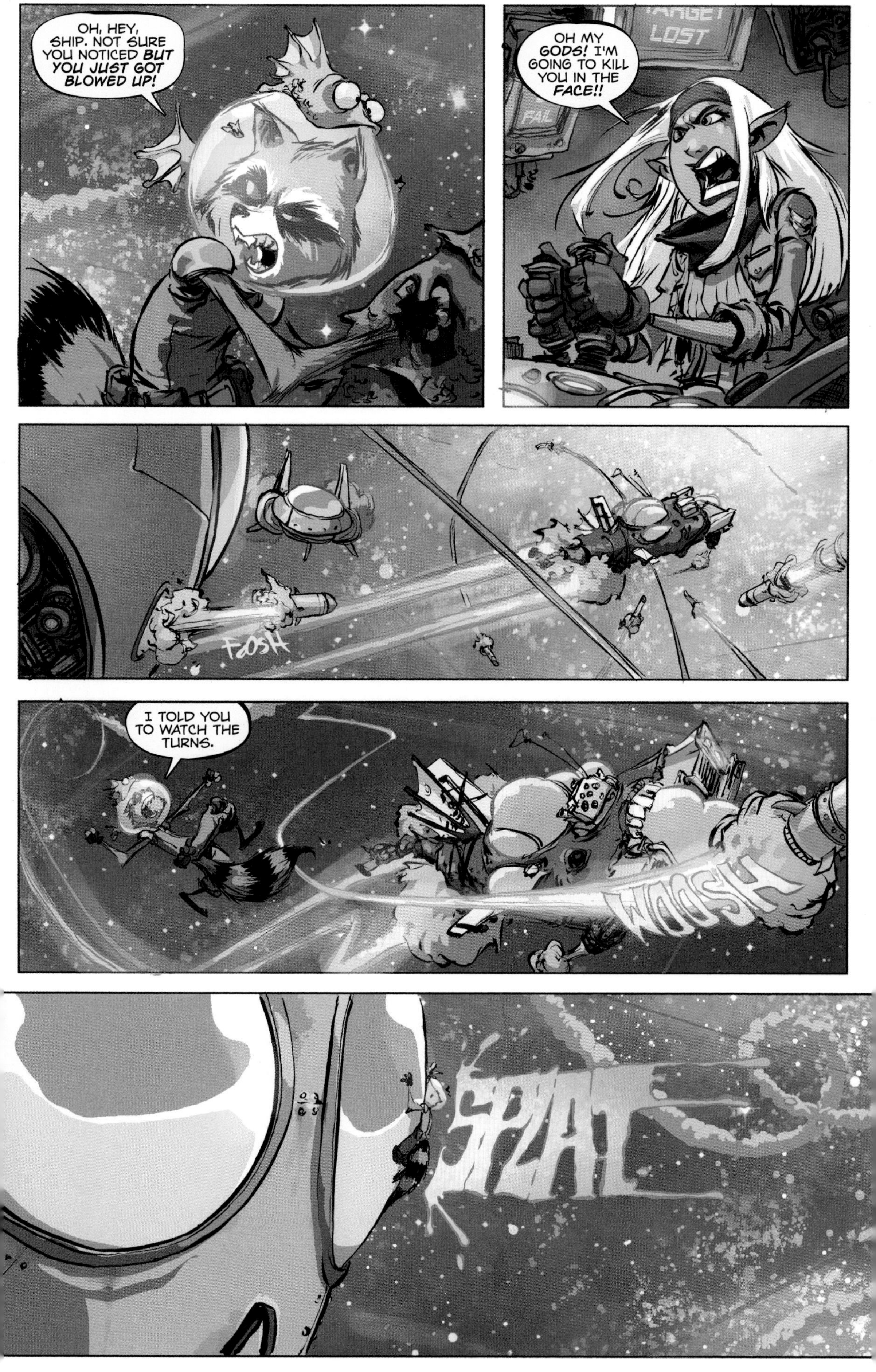
OH, HEY, SHIP. NOT SURE YOU NOTICED **BUT YOU JUST GOT BLOWED UP!**
LOST
FAIL
OH MY ***GODS!*** I'M GOING TO KILL YOU IN THE ***FACE!!***
FOOSH
I TOLD YOU TO WATCH THE TURNS.
WOOSH
SPLAT

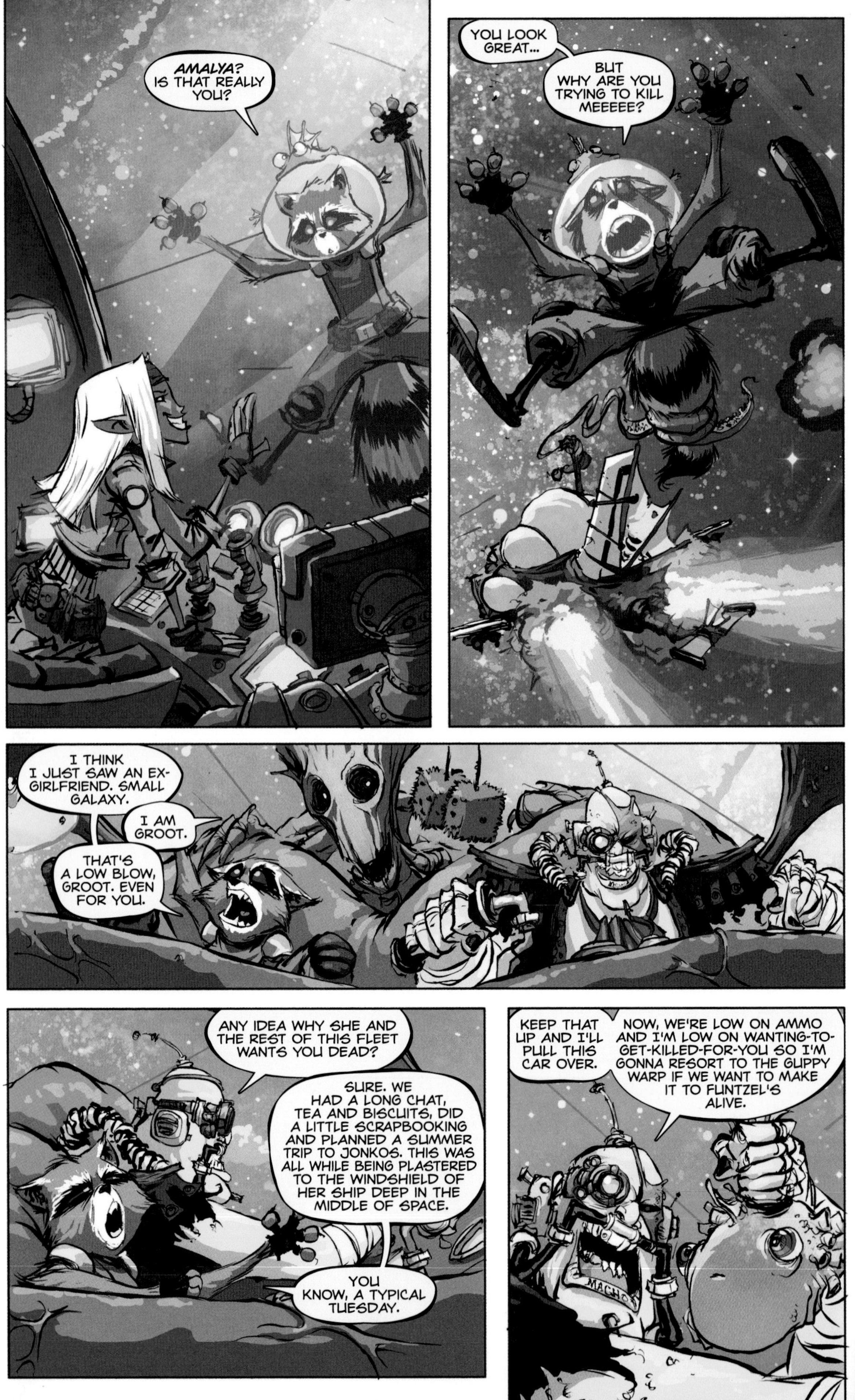
AMALYA? IS THAT REALLY YOU?
YOU LOOK GREAT...
BUT WHY ARE YOU TRYING TO KILL MEEEEE?
I THINK I JUST SAW AN EX-GIRLFRIEND. SMALL GALAXY.
I AM GROOT.
THAT'S A LOW BLOW, GROOT. EVEN FOR YOU.
ANY IDEA WHY SHE AND THE REST OF THIS FLEET WANTS YOU DEAD?
SURE. WE HAD A LONG CHAT, TEA AND BISCUITS, DID A LITTLE SCRAPBOOKING AND PLANNED A SUMMER TRIP TO JONKOS. THIS WAS ALL WHILE BEING PLASTERED TO THE WINDSHIELD OF HER SHIP DEEP IN THE MIDDLE OF SPACE.
YOU KNOW, A TYPICAL TUESDAY.
KEEP THAT UP AND I'LL PULL THIS CAR OVER.
NOW, WE'RE LOW ON AMMO AND I'M LOW ON WANTING-TO-GET-KILLED-FOR-YOU SO I'M GONNA RESORT TO THE GUPPY WARP IF WE WANT TO MAKE IT TO FUNTZEL'S ALIVE.

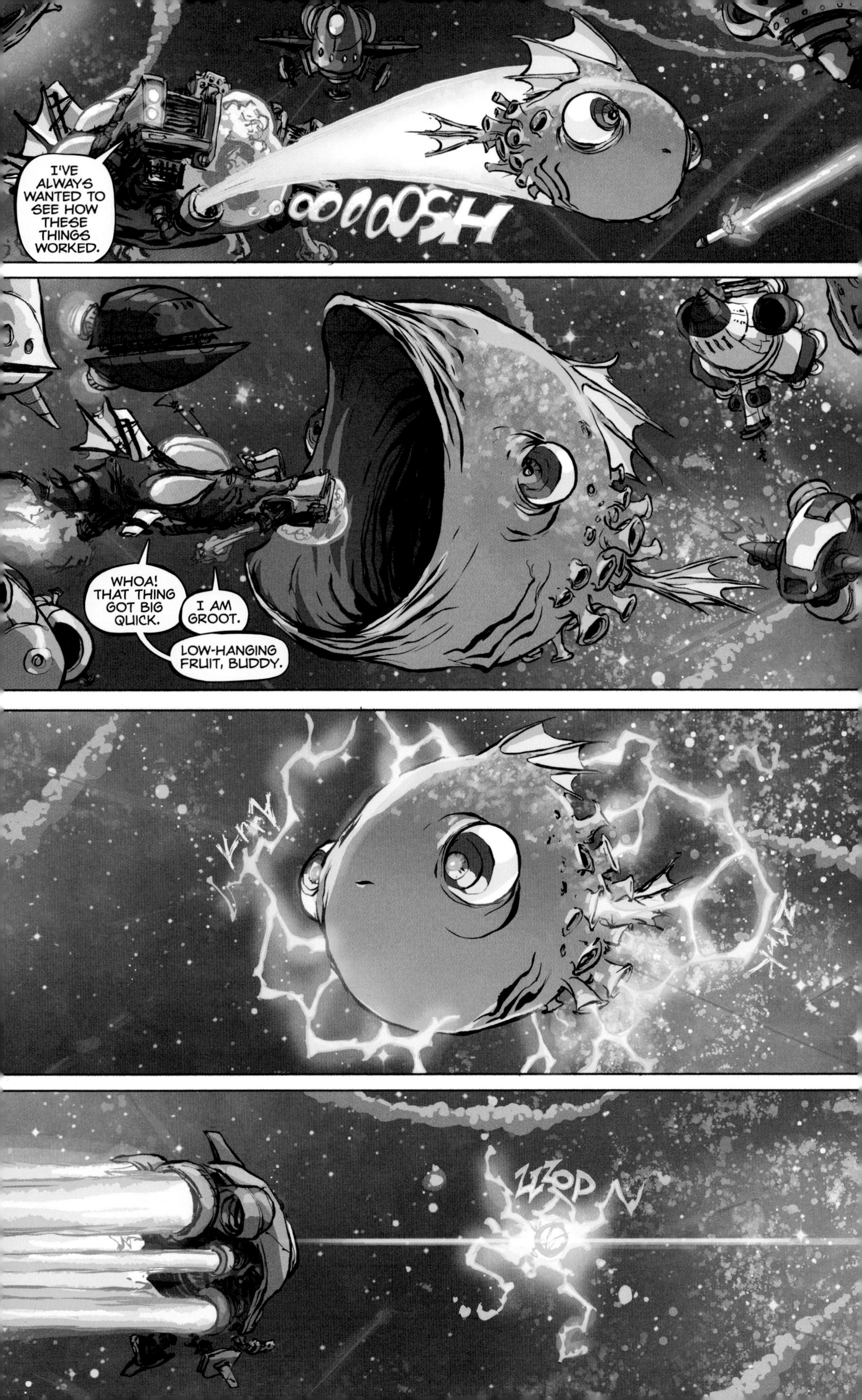
I'VE ALWAYS WANTED TO SEE HOW THESE THINGS WORKED.
WHOA! THAT THING GOT BIG QUICK.
I AM GROOT.
LOW-HANGING FRUIT, BUDDY.

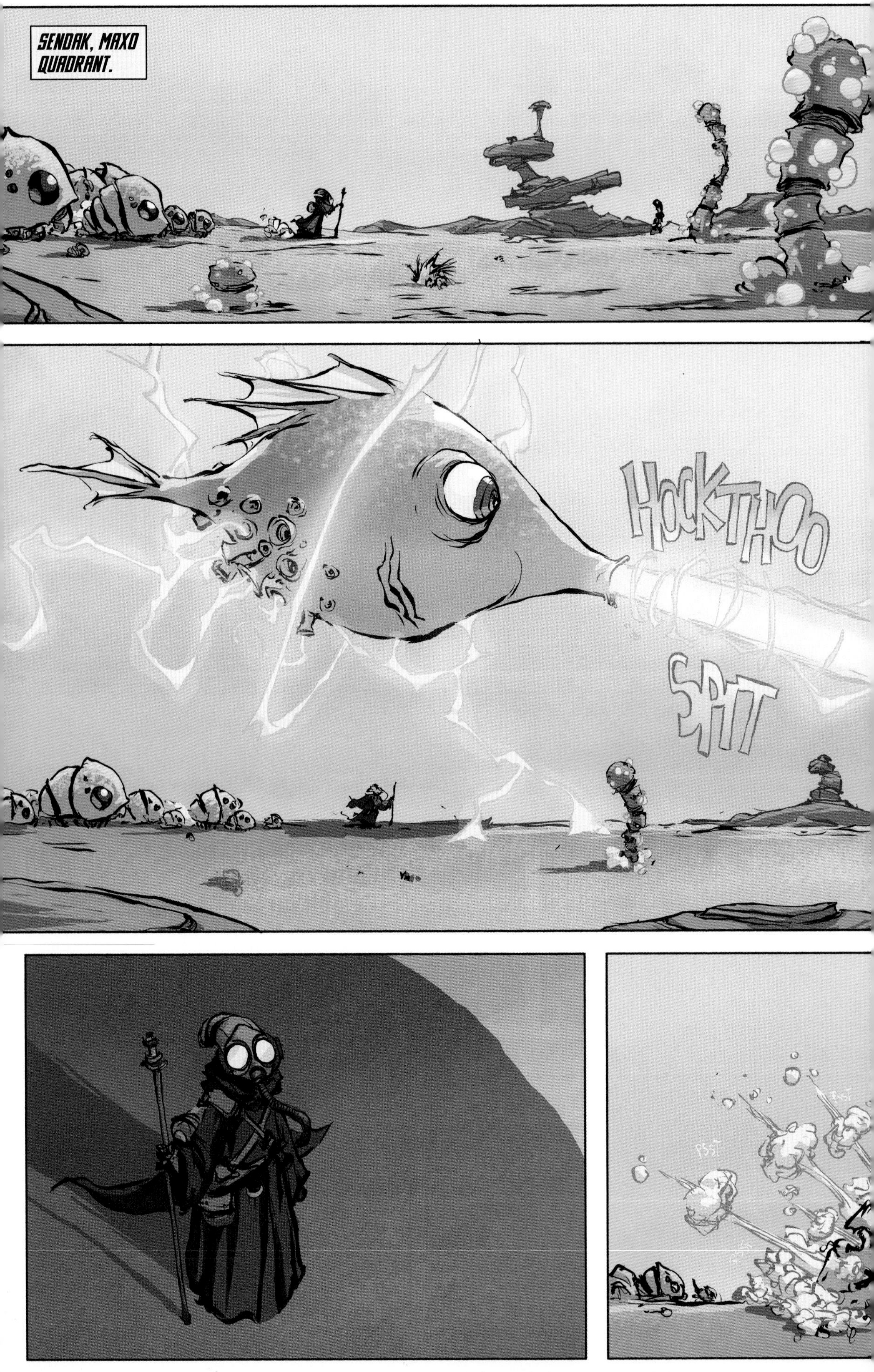
SENDAK, MAXO QUADRANT.
HOCKTHOO
SPIT
PSST
PSST
PSST

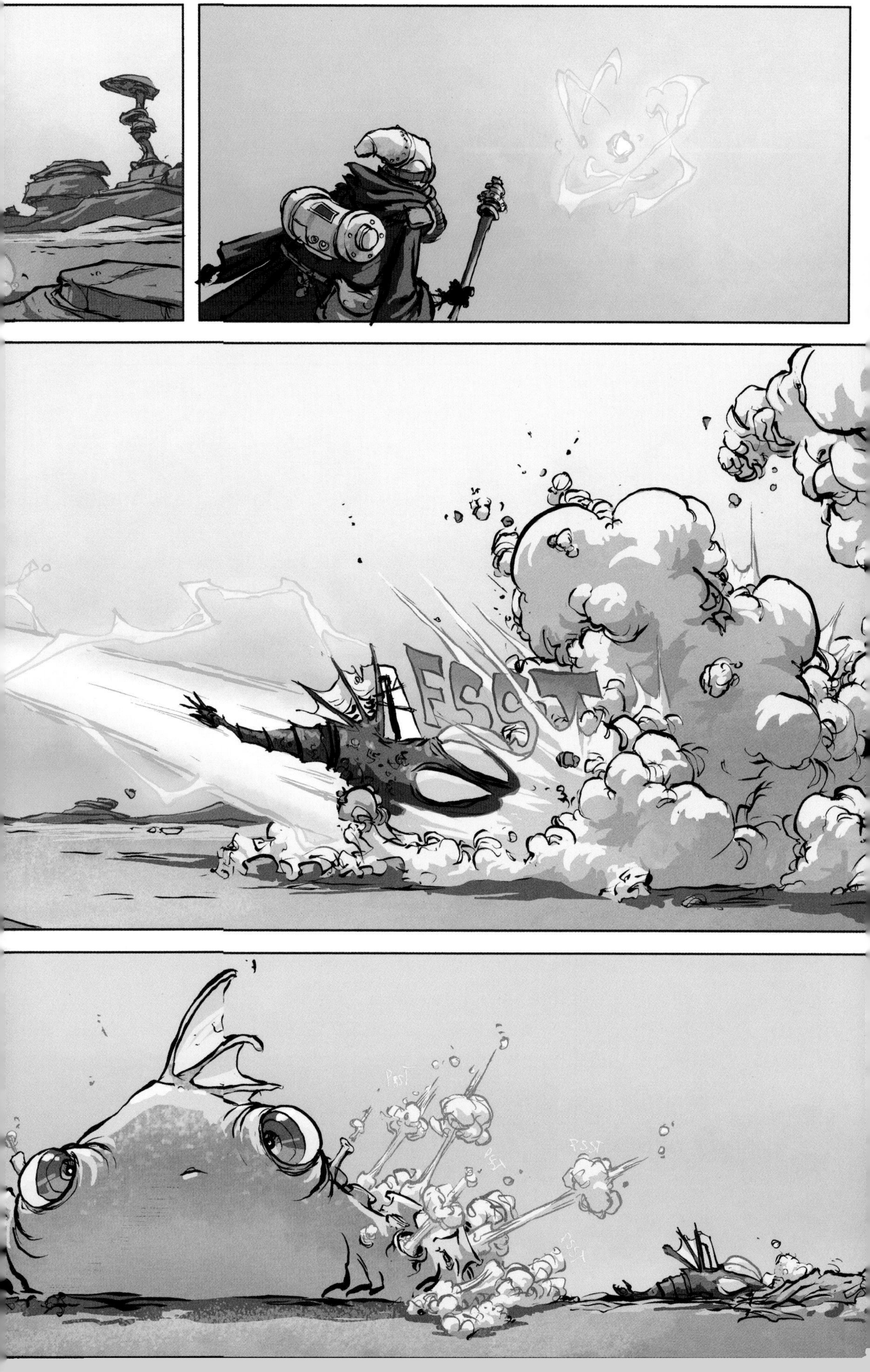
FSST
PSST

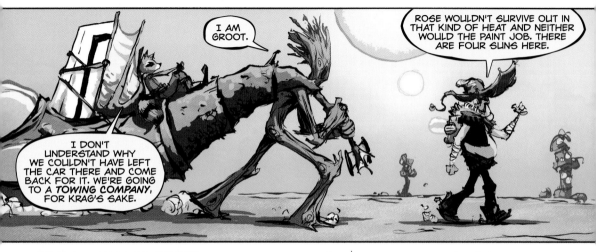

I AM GROOT.

ROSE WOULDN'T SURVIVE OUT IN THAT KIND OF HEAT AND NEITHER WOULD THE PAINT JOB. THERE ARE FOUR SUNS HERE.

I DON'T UNDERSTAND WHY WE COULDN'T HAVE LEFT THE CAR THERE AND COME BACK FOR IT. WE'RE GOING TO A *TOWING COMPANY,* FOR KRAG'S SAKE.

SPEAKING OF HERE, I STILL DON'T SEE HOW FUNTZEL PLAYS INTO ALL OF THIS. YOU MURDERED SOME FOLKS, WHAT DOES HE HAVE TO DO WITH IT?

I TOLD YOU, I'M LOOKING FOR INFORMATION ON WHOEVER'S SETTING ME UP.

TOO SIMPLE AN ANSWER FOR ALL THIS FUSS, AMIGO. I'M NOT BUYING IT.

I'M THE ONE BUYING YOU, SO WHY DON'T YOU DO YOUR JOB AND LEAD THE WAY.

NOBODY BUYS MACHO GOMEZ, MAPACHE.

I AM GROOT!

HUH--

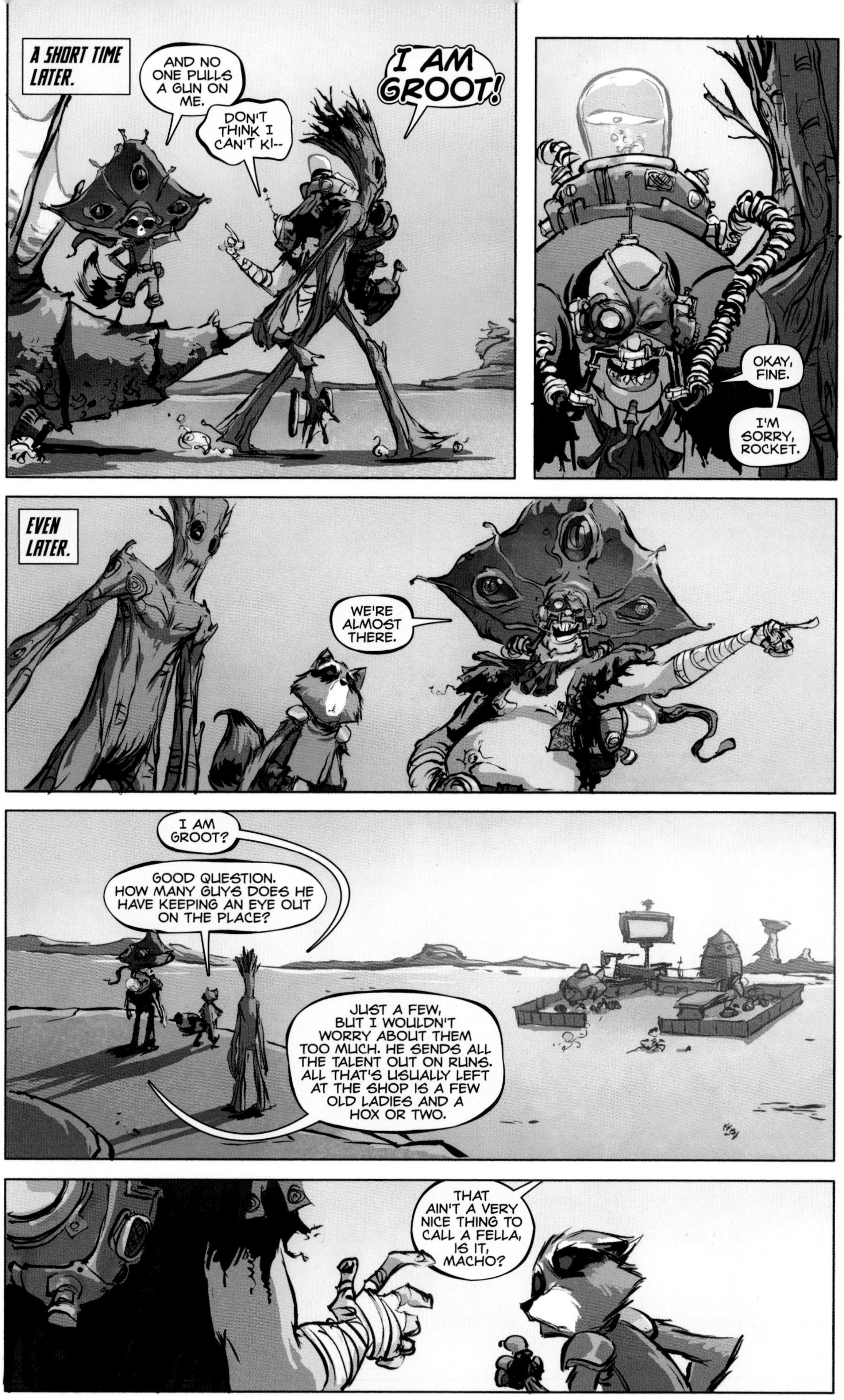
A SHORT TIME LATER.
AND NO ONE PULLS A GUN ON ME.
DON'T THINK I CAN'T KI--
I AM GROOT!
OKAY, FINE.
I'M SORRY, ROCKET.
EVEN LATER.
WE'RE ALMOST THERE.
I AM GROOT?
GOOD QUESTION. HOW MANY GUYS DOES HE HAVE KEEPING AN EYE OUT ON THE PLACE?
JUST A FEW, BUT I WOULDN'T WORRY ABOUT THEM TOO MUCH. HE SENDS ALL THE TALENT OUT ON RUNS. ALL THAT'S USUALLY LEFT AT THE SHOP IS A FEW OLD LADIES AND A HOX OR TWO.
THAT AIN'T A VERY NICE THING TO CALL A FELLA, IS IT, MACHO?

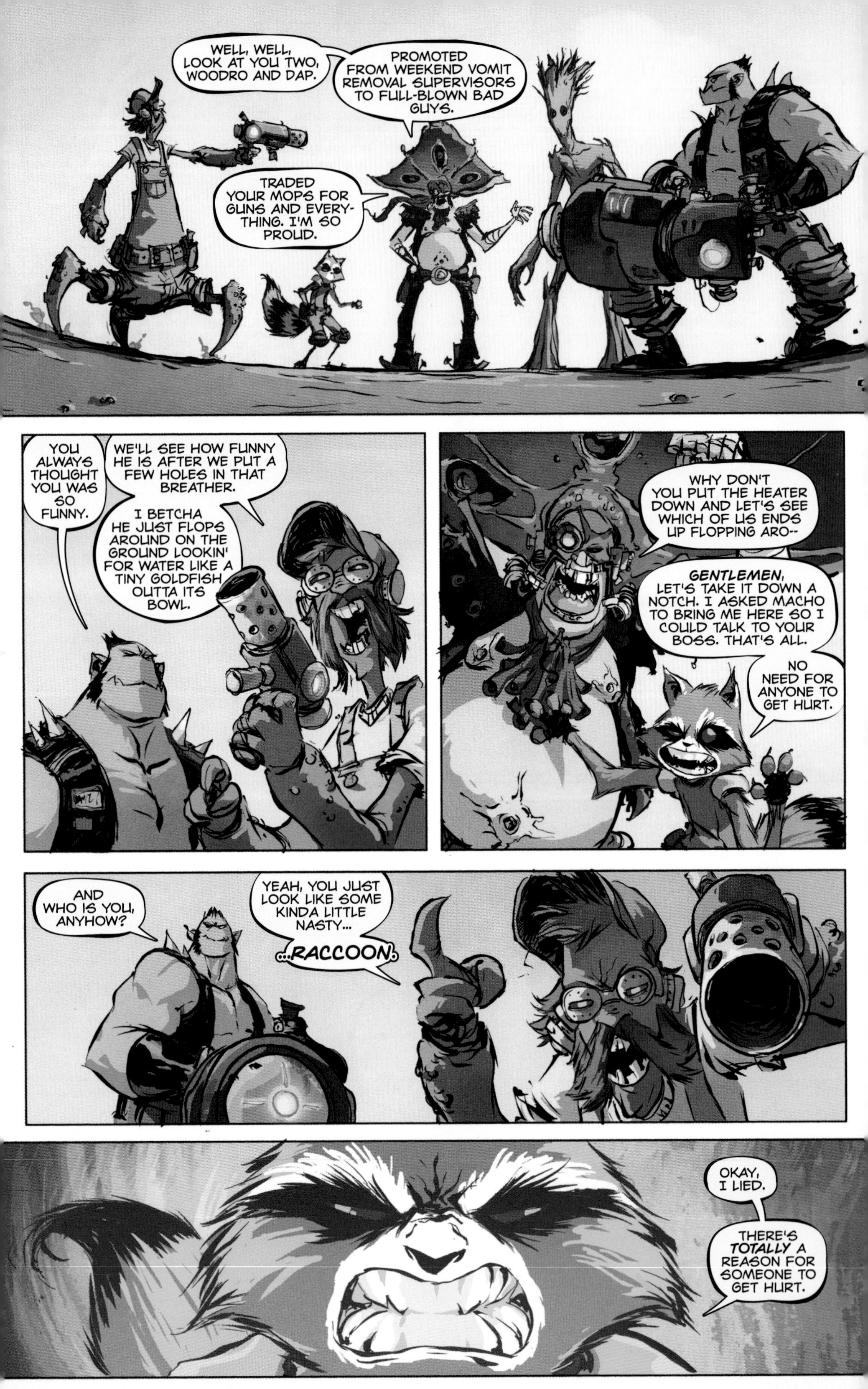
WELL, WELL, LOOK AT YOU TWO, WOODRO AND DAP.
PROMOTED FROM WEEKEND VOMIT REMOVAL SUPERVISORS TO FULL-BLOWN BAD GUYS.
TRADED YOUR MOPS FOR GUNS AND EVERY-THING. I'M SO PROUD.
YOU ALWAYS THOUGHT YOU WAS SO FUNNY.
WE'LL SEE HOW FUNNY HE IS AFTER WE PUT A FEW HOLES IN THAT BREATHER.
I BETCHA HE JUST FLOPS AROUND ON THE GROUND LOOKIN' FOR WATER LIKE A TINY GOLDFISH OUTTA ITS BOWL.
WHY DON'T YOU PUT THE HEATER DOWN AND LET'S SEE WHICH OF US ENDS UP FLOPPING ARO--
GENTLEMEN, LET'S TAKE IT DOWN A NOTCH. I ASKED MACHO TO BRING ME HERE SO I COULD TALK TO YOUR BOSS. THAT'S ALL.
NO NEED FOR ANYONE TO GET HURT.
AND WHO IS YOU, ANYHOW?
YEAH, YOU JUST LOOK LIKE SOME KINDA LITTLE NASTY...
...RACCOON.
OKAY, I LIED.
THERE'S *TOTALLY* A REASON FOR SOMEONE TO GET HURT.

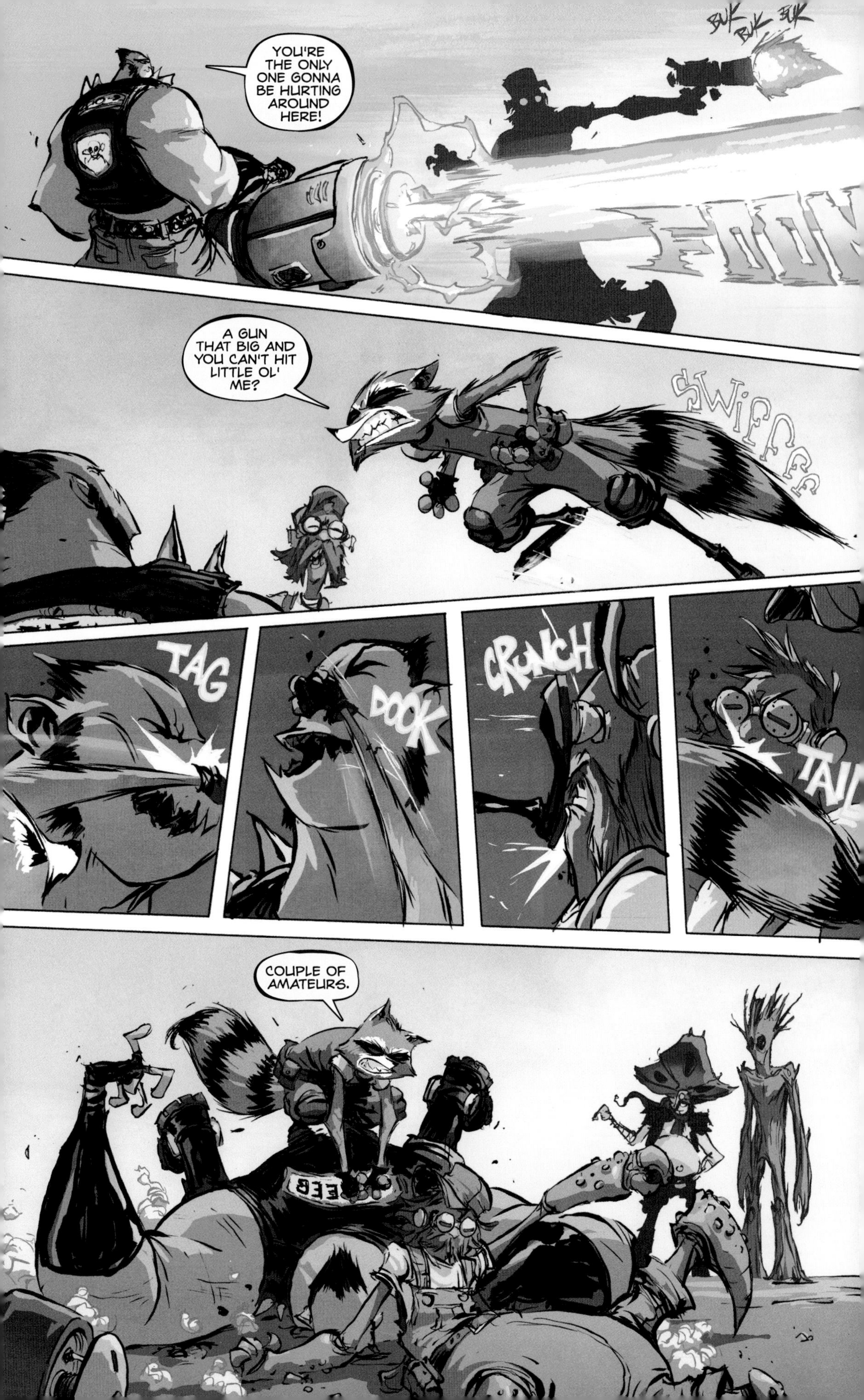

YOU'RE THE ONLY ONE GONNA BE HURTING AROUND HERE!
BUK BUK BUK
A GUN THAT BIG AND YOU CAN'T HIT LITTLE OL' ME?
SWIFFFF
TAG
DOOK
CRUNCH
TAIL
COUPLE OF AMATEURS.

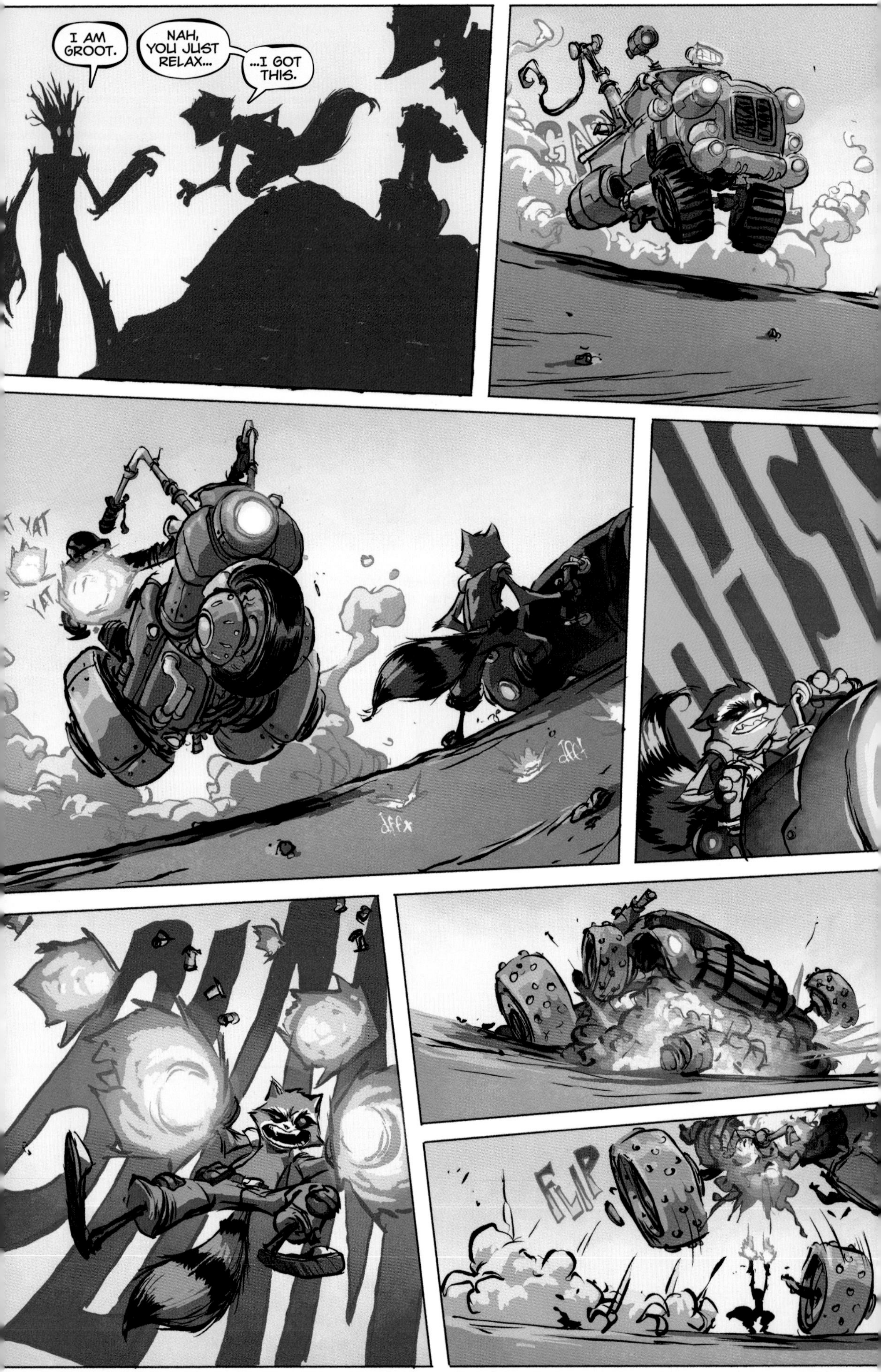
I AM GROOT.
NAH, YOU JUST RELAX...
...I GOT THIS.
YAT
YAT
FLIP

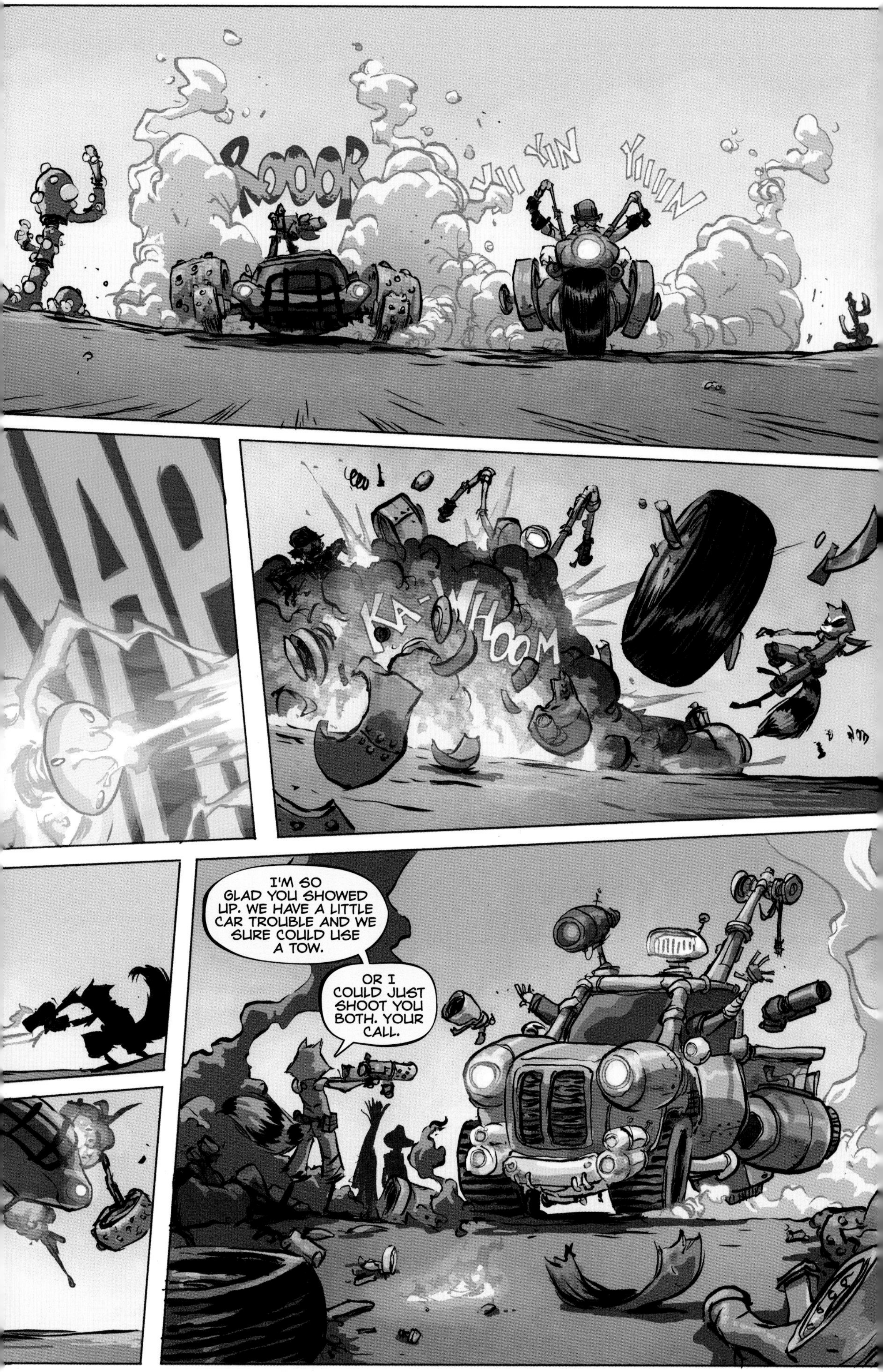
ROOOR
YIIIN YIIN
YIIIIN
KA-WHOOM
I'M SO GLAD YOU SHOWED UP. WE HAVE A LITTLE CAR TROUBLE AND WE SURE COULD USE A TOW.
OR I COULD JUST SHOOT YOU BOTH. YOUR CALL.

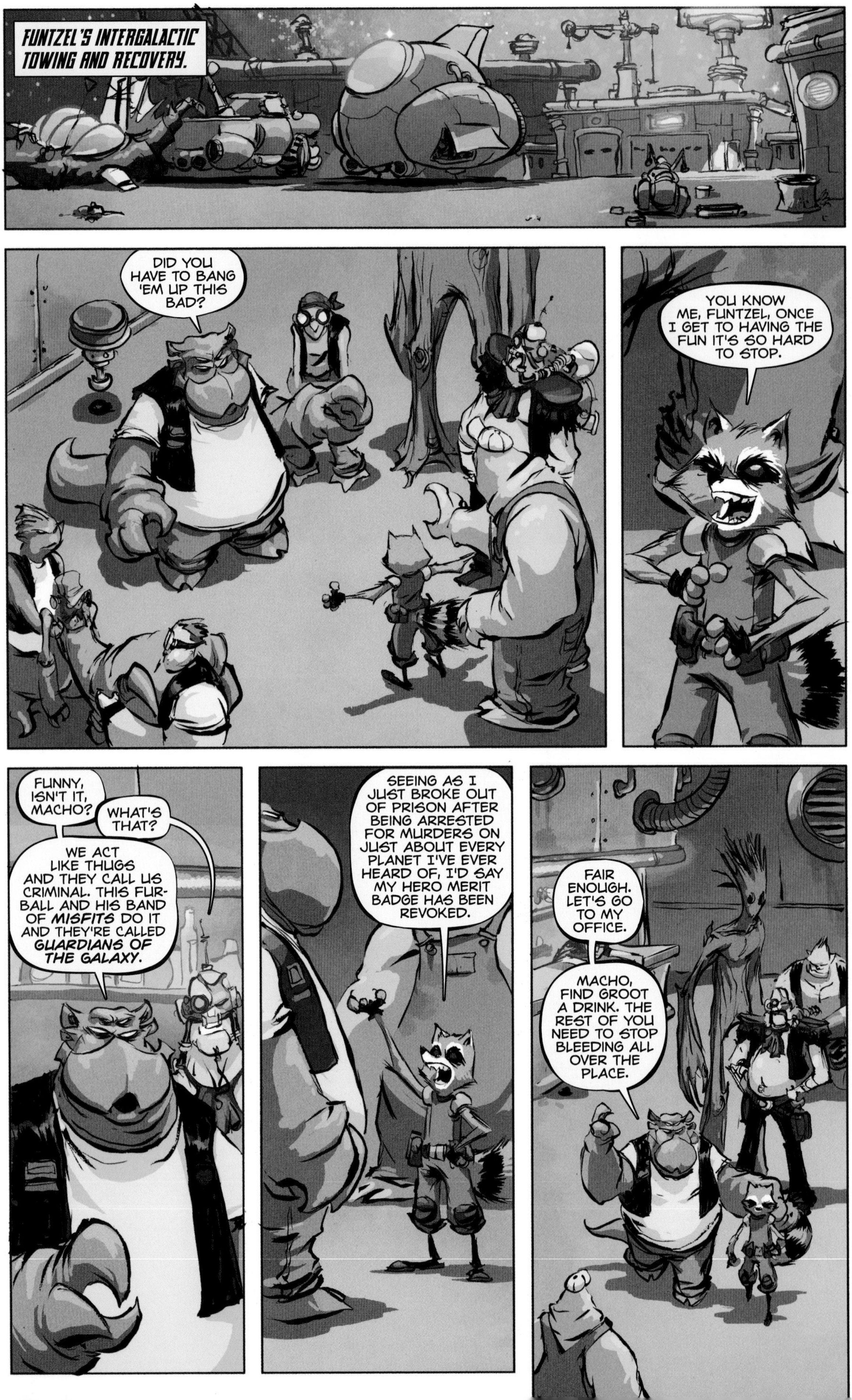
FUNTZEL'S INTERGALACTIC TOWING AND RECOVERY.
DID YOU HAVE TO BANG 'EM UP THIS BAD?
YOU KNOW ME, FUNTZEL, ONCE I GET TO HAVING THE FUN IT'S SO HARD TO STOP.
FUNNY, ISN'T IT, MACHO?
WHAT'S THAT?
WE ACT LIKE THUGS AND THEY CALL US CRIMINAL. THIS FURBALL AND HIS BAND OF MISFITS DO IT AND THEY'RE CALLED GUARDIANS OF THE GALAXY.
SEEING AS I JUST BROKE OUT OF PRISON AFTER BEING ARRESTED FOR MURDERS ON JUST ABOUT EVERY PLANET I'VE EVER HEARD OF, I'D SAY MY HERO MERIT BADGE HAS BEEN REVOKED.
FAIR ENOUGH. LET'S GO TO MY OFFICE.
MACHO, FIND GROOT A DRINK. THE REST OF YOU NEED TO STOP BLEEDING ALL OVER THE PLACE.

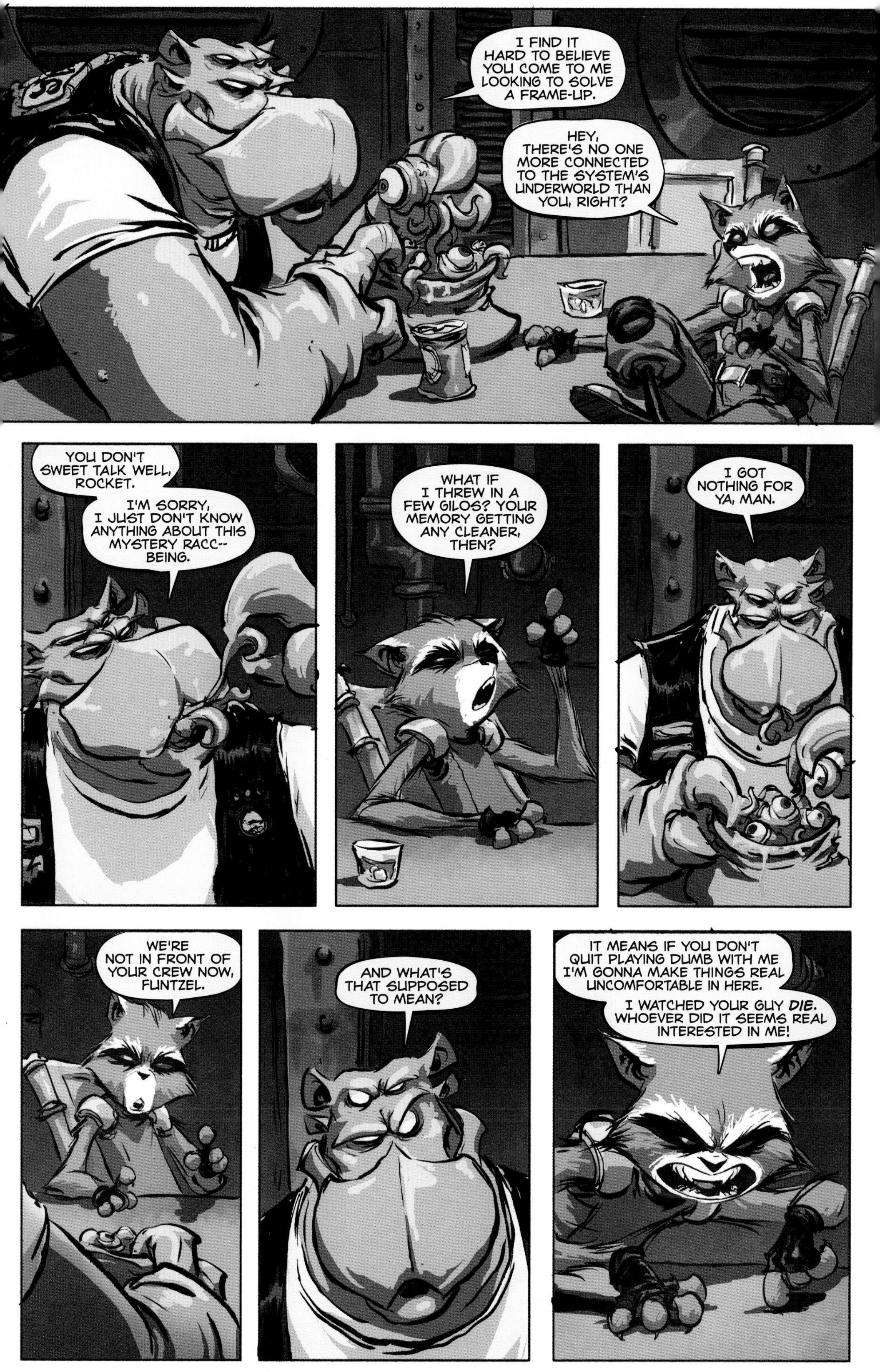
I FIND IT HARD TO BELIEVE YOU COME TO ME LOOKING TO SOLVE A FRAME-UP.
HEY, THERE'S NO ONE MORE CONNECTED TO THE SYSTEM'S UNDERWORLD THAN YOU, RIGHT?
YOU DON'T SWEET TALK WELL, ROCKET.
I'M SORRY, I JUST DON'T KNOW ANYTHING ABOUT THIS MYSTERY RACC-- BEING.
WHAT IF I THREW IN A FEW GILOS? YOUR MEMORY GETTING ANY CLEANER, THEN?
I GOT NOTHING FOR YA, MAN.
WE'RE NOT IN FRONT OF YOUR CREW NOW, FUNTZEL.
AND WHAT'S THAT SUPPOSED TO MEAN?
IT MEANS IF YOU DON'T QUIT PLAYING DUMB WITH ME I'M GONNA MAKE THINGS REAL UNCOMFORTABLE IN HERE.
I WATCHED YOUR GUY *DIE*. WHOEVER DID IT SEEMS REAL INTERESTED IN ME!

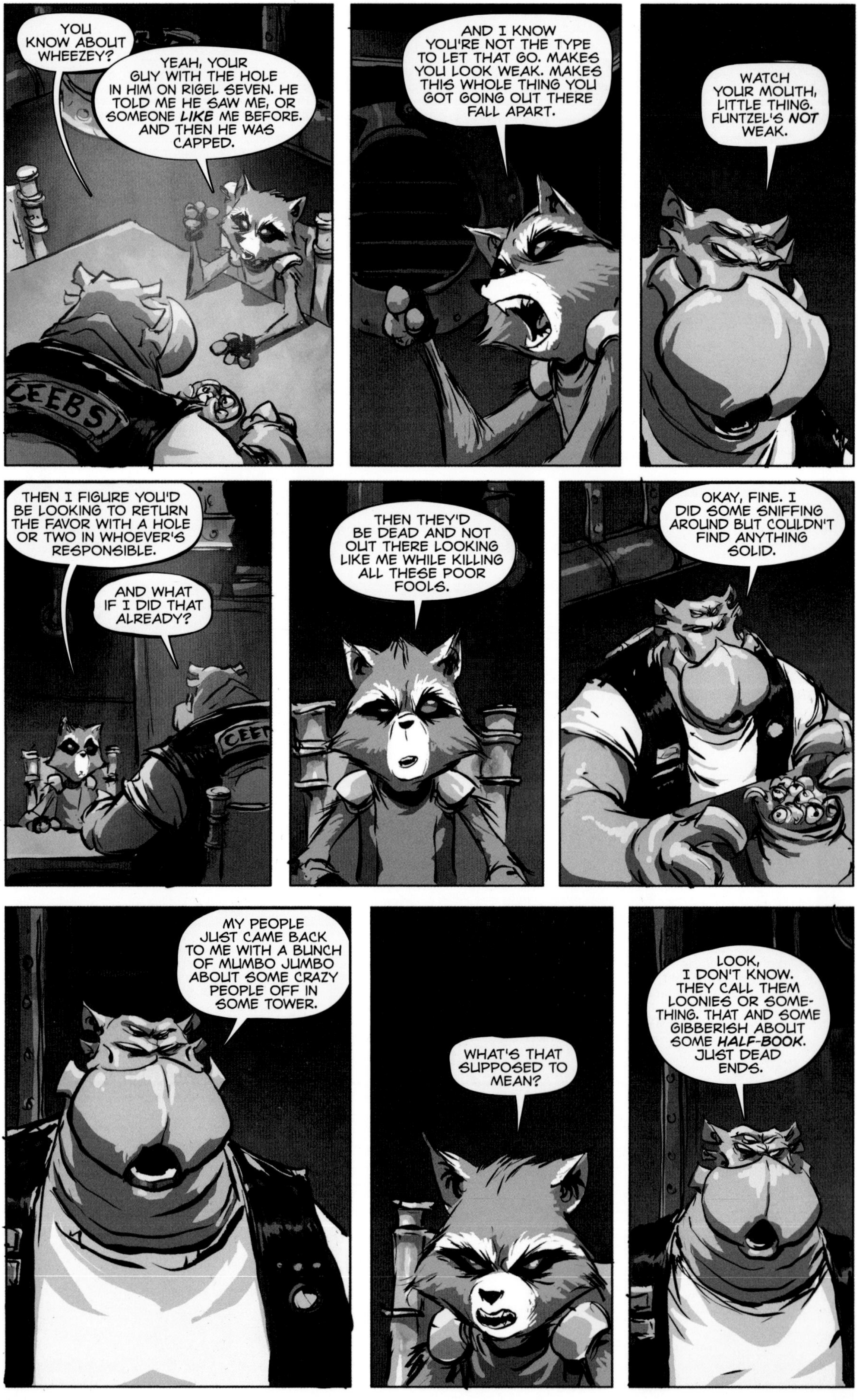
YOU KNOW ABOUT WHEEZEY?
YEAH, YOUR GUY WITH THE HOLE IN HIM ON RIGEL SEVEN. HE TOLD ME HE SAW ME, OR SOMEONE LIKE ME BEFORE. AND THEN HE WAS CAPPED.
CEEBS
AND I KNOW YOU'RE NOT THE TYPE TO LET THAT GO. MAKES YOU LOOK WEAK. MAKES THIS WHOLE THING YOU GOT GOING OUT THERE FALL APART.
WATCH YOUR MOUTH, LITTLE THING. FUNTZEL'S NOT WEAK.
THEN I FIGURE YOU'D BE LOOKING TO RETURN THE FAVOR WITH A HOLE OR TWO IN WHOEVER'S RESPONSIBLE.
AND WHAT IF I DID THAT ALREADY?
THEN THEY'D BE DEAD AND NOT OUT THERE LOOKING LIKE ME WHILE KILLING ALL THESE POOR FOOLS.
OKAY, FINE. I DID SOME SNIFFING AROUND BUT COULDN'T FIND ANYTHING SOLID.
MY PEOPLE JUST CAME BACK TO ME WITH A BUNCH OF MUMBO JUMBO ABOUT SOME CRAZY PEOPLE OFF IN SOME TOWER.
WHAT'S THAT SUPPOSED TO MEAN?
LOOK, I DON'T KNOW. THEY CALL THEM LOONIES OR SOMETHING. THAT AND SOME GIBBERISH ABOUT SOME HALF-BOOK. JUST DEAD ENDS.

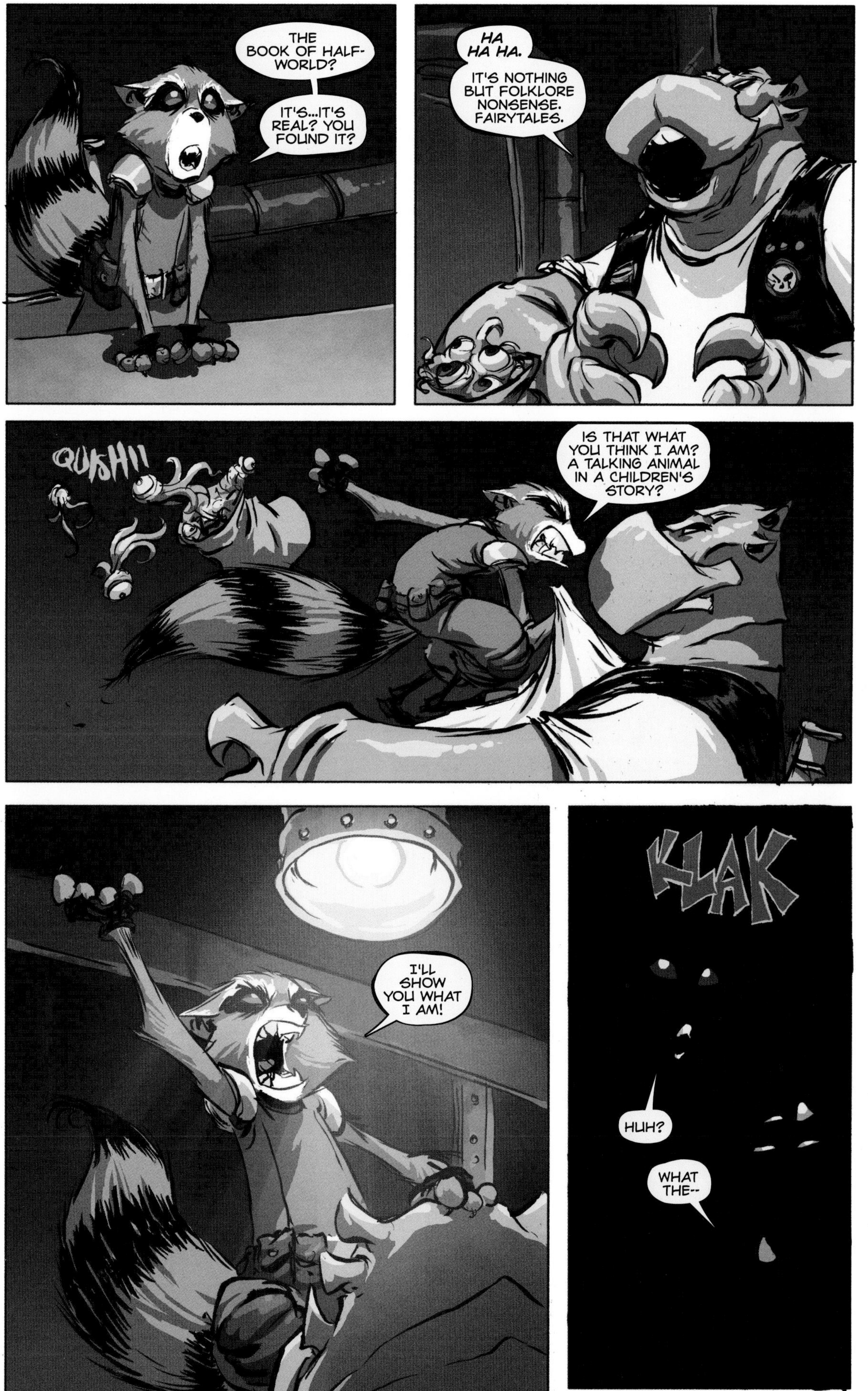
THE BOOK OF HALF-WORLD?
IT'S...IT'S REAL? YOU FOUND IT?
HA HA HA.
IT'S NOTHING BUT FOLKLORE NONSENSE. FAIRYTALES.
QUISH!!
IS THAT WHAT YOU THINK I AM? A TALKING ANIMAL IN A CHILDREN'S STORY?
I'LL SHOW YOU WHAT I AM!
KLAK
HUH?
WHAT THE--

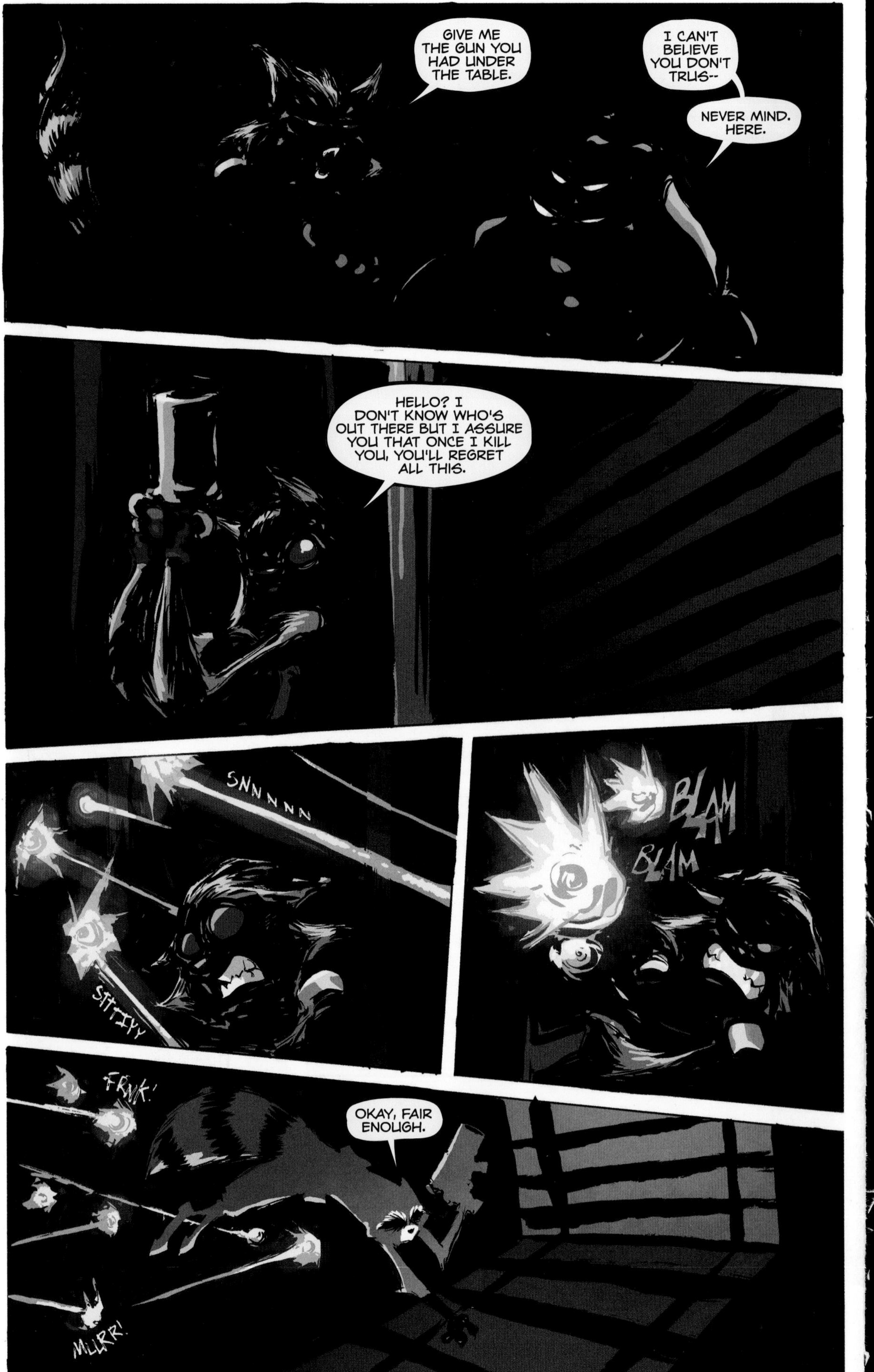
GIVE ME THE GUN YOU HAD UNDER THE TABLE.
I CAN'T BELIEVE YOU DON'T TRUS--
NEVER MIND. HERE.
HELLO? I DON'T KNOW WHO'S OUT THERE BUT I ASSURE YOU THAT ONCE I KILL YOU, YOU'LL REGRET ALL THIS.
SNNNNNN
STTTYYY
BLAM
BLAM
FRNK!
OKAY, FAIR ENOUGH.
MLLRR!

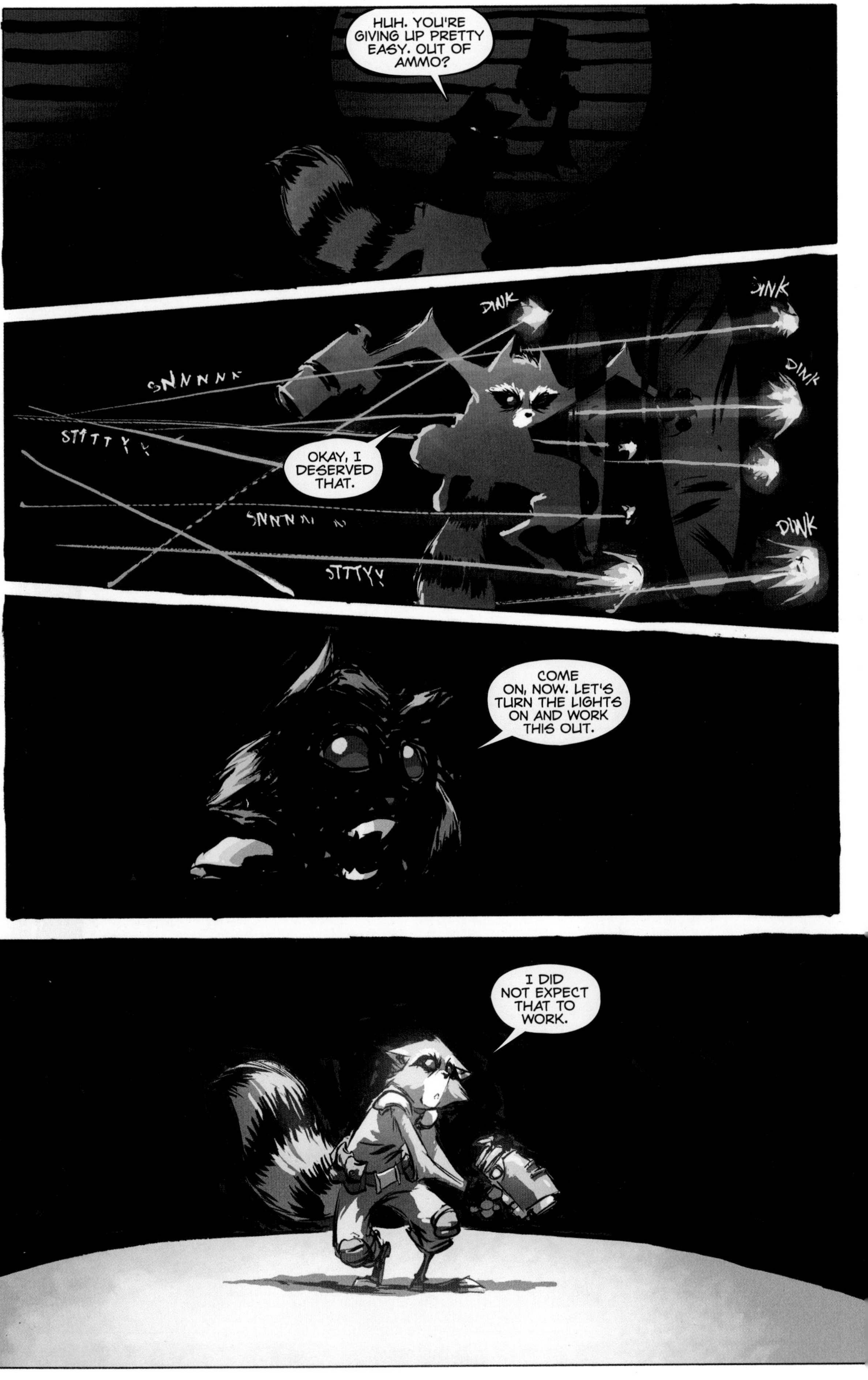
HUH. YOU'RE GIVING UP PRETTY EASY. OUT OF AMMO?
DINK
DINK
DINK
OKAY, I DESERVED THAT.
DINK
COME ON, NOW. LET'S TURN THE LIGHTS ON AND WORK THIS OUT.
I DID NOT EXPECT THAT TO WORK.

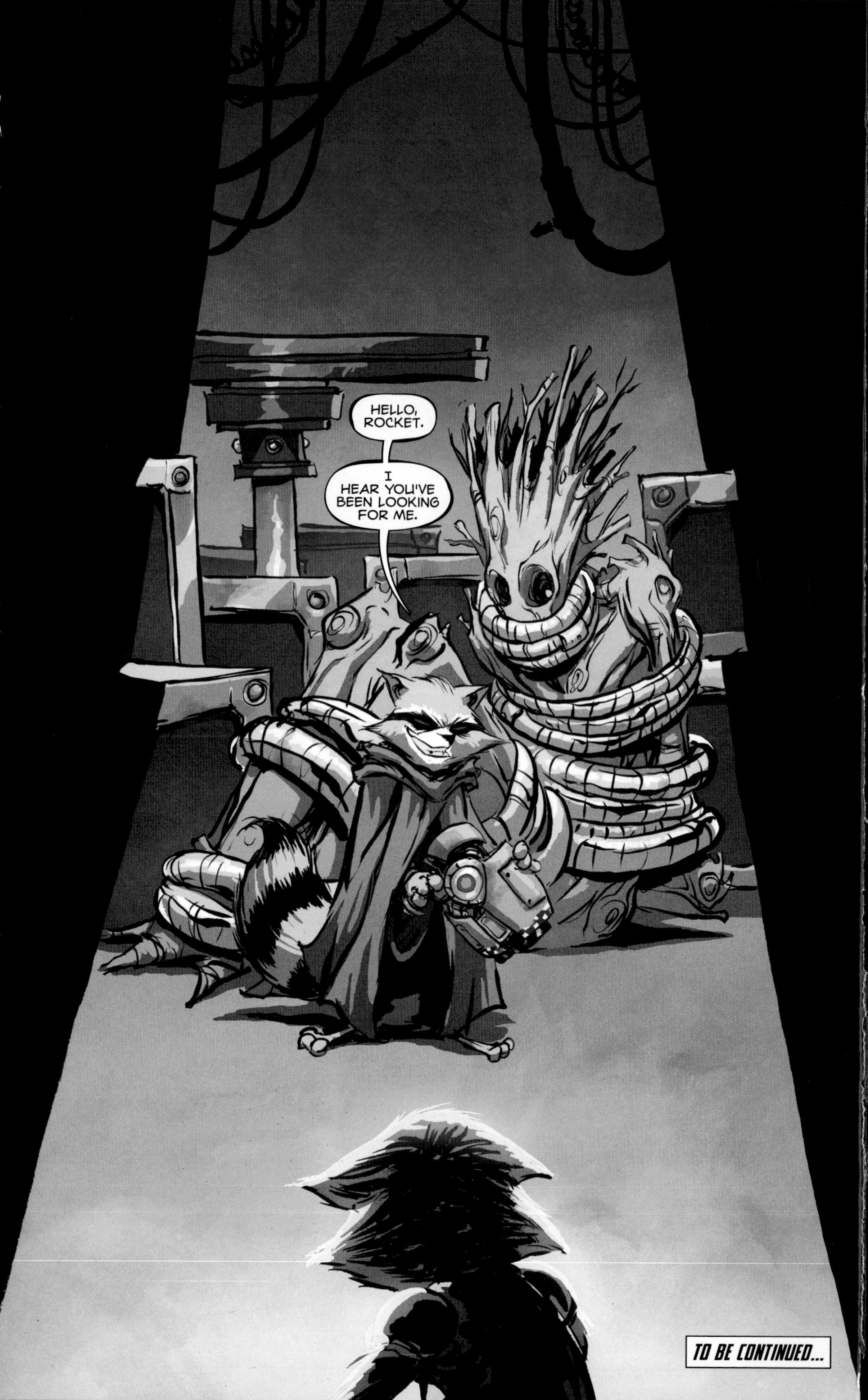
HELLO, ROCKET.
I HEAR YOU'VE BEEN LOOKING FOR ME.
TO BE CONTINUED...